BUB

or THE VERY BEST THING

NATALIE BABBITT

Michael di Capua Books ◆ *HarperCollins Publishers*

BUB

or THE VERY BEST THING

This book is for all the dear and patient people

—not to mention the dog—

whose faces appear in its pages

One day in the castle the King and the Queen had an argument.

"You give the Prince too many toys," said the King. "If this keeps up, he'll turn out soft and silly."

"You give the Prince too many lessons," said the Queen. "If that keeps up, he'll turn out dry and dusty."

"I only want what's best for him," said the King.

"But that's what I want, too," said the Queen.

"See here," said the King. "If we both want what's best for him, there's nothing to argue about."

"You're right, my love," said the Queen.

And the King gave the Queen a kiss.

"Bub," said the Prince.

"But," said the Queen, "what *is* the best thing for him? The one and only very best thing."

"I'm not at all sure," said the King. "Are you?"

"No," said the Queen, "I'm not."

"You can find out anything from books," said the King. "I'll get the Prime Minister to help me look."

"All right," said the Queen. "And while you're doing that, the Prince and I will take a walk about."

So the King and the Prime Minister settled down to look up the question in books, and the Queen and the Prince went away through the castle.

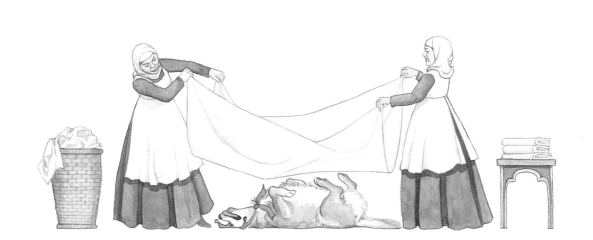

They hadn't gone far before they found the Day and Night Nursemaids.

"Well, now," said the Queen, "since we've met like this, I don't suppose you know what's the best thing for His Highness, the Prince?"

"Vegetables," said the Day Nursemaid.

"And plenty of sleep," said the Night Nursemaid.

"Vegetables and sleep!" said the Queen.

"Absolutely," said the Day Nursemaid. "Unless you don't want him to be strong."

"Of course I do," said the Queen. "But neither of those could be the *one* and only very best thing."

"He wouldn't get far without them," said the Night Nursemaid. "But don't listen to us."

So the Queen and the Prince didn't listen. They went along and looked out a window, and there was the Castle Gardener trimming the ivy.

"Hello," said the Queen. "And by the way, I don't suppose you'd know what's the best thing for His Highness, the Prince?"

"Sunshine," said the Gardener.

"Sunshine!" said the Queen.

"Certainly," said the Gardener. "All growing things need sunshine. Do you want him to grow or don't you?"

"Of course I do," said the Queen. "But sunshine can't be the one and *only* very best thing."

"He wouldn't get far without it," said the Gardener. "But suit yourself."

So the Queen and the Prince suited themselves and went on till they found the Court Musician playing his lute.

"Good day," said the Queen. "And while we're all together here, I don't suppose you'd know what's the best thing for His Highness, the Prince?"

"A song," said the Court Musician.

"What song?" said the Queen.

"Any song," said the Court Musician. "All songs. Sad, happy, and in between. Songs explain the heart. He has a heart, doesn't he?"

"Of course he does," said the Queen. "But songs can't be the one and only *very* best thing."

"He wouldn't get far without them," said the Court Musician. "But have it your own way."

So the Queen and the Prince had it their own way and went on till they met a Lord and a Lady.

"Here you are," said the Queen. "And since I'm asking everyone, I don't suppose you'd know what's the best thing for His Highness, the Prince?"

"Talk to him," said the Lord, "and listen."

"Talk and listen!" said the Queen.

"No doubt about it," said the Lady. "If you want to understand him."

"Of course I do," said the Queen. "But talking and listening can't be the one and only very *best* thing."

"He wouldn't get far without them," said the Lord. "But pay no attention to us."

So the Queen and the Prince paid no attention. They walked on through the castle and soon the King came to find them.

"Well, my love," said the Queen, "did your books have the answer to our question?"

"No," said the King. "They all said something different."

"That's how it was with the people I spoke to," said the Queen. "Perhaps there isn't any answer."

While they were talking it over, they wandered to the bottom of the castle and there was the Cook's Daughter.

"How do you do," said the King.

"And as long as we're here," said the Queen, "I might as well ask if you know what's the best thing for His Highness, the Prince."

"What!" said the Cook's Daughter. "Don't you know?"

"We're not exactly sure," said the King.

"Did you try asking the Prince?" said the Cook's Daughter.

"We didn't think of that," said the King.

"Well, for goodness' sake," said the Cook's Daughter. "Here. I'll ask him. But I know what he'll say."

She whispered in the Prince's ear and the Prince whispered back. "There's your answer," said the Cook's Daughter. "The one and only very best thing is bub."

"Bub!" said the Queen.

"What does it mean?" said the King.

"I have to peel potatoes now," said the Cook's Daughter. "Goodbye."

So the King and the Queen and the Prince started back through the castle. "I guess it doesn't matter what the best thing is," said the Queen, "as long as he knows how much we dote on him." And she knelt down and gave the Prince a kiss.

"Bub," said the Prince.

"I've got it!" said the King. "That word—it must mean *hug*."

"Oh, I don't think so," said the Queen.

"Well, maybe not," said the King.

"One of these days," said the Queen, "he'll be able to explain it to us himself."

"True enough," said the King. "Just think of that!"

So they went and had muffins and strawberry jam and everyone was happy.

Everyone.

And the Cook's Daughter said
to the Cook, "The Prince was right, Mama.
Love *is* the very best thing."